Better Off WITHOUT Me

HARRIETTE CORET

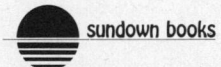

New Readers Press • Syracuse, New York

This novel is a work of fiction. Names, characters, places, and incidents either are the products of the author's imagination or are used fictitiously, and any resemblance to actual persons, living or dead, events, or locales is entirely coincidental.

ISBN 0-88336-762-9

© 1989

New Readers Press

Publishing Division of Laubach Literacy International

Box 131, Syracuse, New York 13210

All rights reserved. No part of this book may be reproduced or transmitted in any form or by any means, electronic or mechanical, including photocopying, recording, or by any information storage and retrieval system, without permission in writing from the publisher.

Printed in the United States of America

Edited by Annie Billups
Illustrations by Fran Forstadt
Cover design by Chris Steenwerth
Cover illustration by Fran Forstadt

9 8 7 6 5 4 3 2

For Eva Karin

Chapter 1

Elsa Caukins leaned against the kitchen sink. Yes, she thought, it's the only way out. I'll do it. But where? And when? And how? Her hand slowly brought a cigarette to her lips. She drew on it. Then her other hand brought a glass to her mouth. She drank. The children mustn't find me afterwards, she thought. And I can't involve Bill. Maybe I should write a note. No, there's nothing to say.

If she had been listening, Elsa would have heard Bill's truck pull into the driveway. But Elsa didn't listen well anymore. It wasn't until Bill opened the door that she noticed his arrival.

"Hi, sweetheart," he called out. Then he saw the bottle on the drainboard. And the glass in Elsa's hand. "Must you?" He frowned and avoided Elsa's eyes.

Elsa corked the bottle and put it into the cupboard. "It's such a struggle getting through the day."

"Look," Bill said. "I know you're going through a hard time. But some of the things you do make it worse. Worse for you and worse for me." His voice began to rise. "Look at this floor. Look at the stove. You haven't even cleared the kids' supper from the table. I'm tired, Elsa, and I'm hungry. How do you think I feel when I walk in here at night? There's no dinner, no kiss. When do I get taken care of?"

"I know." Elsa began to sob.

Bill put his arms around her. "I've been thinking. Kevin will be out of school in a few days. Why don't you take the kids and go visit your mother?"

"No, I can't."

Bill chose his words carefully. "I don't know how much more I can take, Elsa. A year ago, when we bought the gas station, you were OK. You were going to help. And you did help, at first. But now I have to do my work and yours, too. I'm not Superman, Elsa."

"I'm sorry." Elsa turned her back and blew her nose. "You'd be better off without me."

"What kind of talk is that? Go visit your mother. Get a good rest. Your mother's crazy about the kids. She's always asking you to bring them."

Elsa stared out the window. Yes, Bill was right. Mom was better with the kids than she was. Why not go to Florida to visit Mom? And why not do it there? The kids would already be used to Mom. Bill couldn't be blamed. Yes. Why hadn't she thought of it herself?

"All right," she said. "I'll go."

Now she knew *where*. *When* and *how* would probably fall into place.

Chapter 2

"I need more sleeping pills," Elsa told her newest doctor.

The doctor paused. He looked at Elsa's record on his desk. "I prescribed pills last time. Did you use them all?"

"Yes, I did," Elsa lied.

"Then you are taking too many. Mrs. Caukins, I cannot prescribe sleeping pills time after time. If you're still depressed, you must see a psychiatrist."

"I can't start with a psychiatrist now. I am going away. I need some pills to tide me over."

"Do you mean you're leaving town?"

"To visit my mother in Florida."

"Oh, I see."

"What did you think I meant?"

"Sometimes a depressed person says she's going away and she means forever. That she's going to..."

"Kill herself? Do you think I'd do that, Doctor?"

The doctor shrugged. "Well, if a person becomes depressed enough.... I'm not trained to judge the depth of your depression, Mrs. Caukins. You really should see a specialist."

"If I could just get some sleep. I have no energy. I'm tired all the time."

"Of course. The depression saps your strength. You can't sleep. You don't eat. If you would treat the depression..."

"I will. Just give me enough pills to last a couple of weeks. Please."

"No, I'm sorry, Mrs. Caukins. I can't do that."

As she headed home, Elsa worried. Did she have enough pills saved up? How many would she need? She didn't know. Those few extra would have been nice.

Chapter 3

Getting ready to go was hard. Phoning Mother. Buying tickets. Deciding what to take. Finding suitcases to take it all in. Many times in the next two weeks Elsa screamed at the children. Or wept. Or had to take a drink.

A few days before she left, Don Gibbons called. Elsa cringed when she heard his voice on the phone. "I told you it's all over between us. Besides, I'm going away."

"Where?"

"To my mother's in Miami."

"What's her phone number?"

"Don, leave me alone. I don't want to hear from you."

"Your mom married again?"

"No."

"One thing about me, Elsa. I've got a good memory. Your mom is Florence Rose. Mrs. Albert Rose, if she still uses your dad's name. Don't worry, I can look it up. I'll come see you, Elsa."

"Please don't, Don." Elsa hung up. But she was shaking and had to lie down for a while. Why had she ever taken up with Don? He was married. She was married. When they were teenagers he had pursued her. But she'd never liked him as a boyfriend. Why, when she ran into him downtown a few months ago, had she let him buy her a drink? And accepted dates with him? And been intimate with him? Why, when she didn't even like him? I must be crazy for sure, she thought.

The night before she and the children left, Bill had to do all the packing. He fed and dressed the children in the morning, too.

Now she was finally on the plane. Her head felt light and her hands shook as the plane began its descent to Miami. We're landing, she thought. Her heart thumped. Now I'll have to face Mom. She'll judge me. Then she'll say, "You have no reason to be unhappy, Elsa. Life has been good to you. Pull yourself together." That's the way it will look to her.

Getting off the plane with three children was a struggle. Elsa carried 10-month-old Abby on one arm. The diaper bag was heavy with baby bottles. Elsa slung it over her shoulder and hung her heavy purse from her wrist. She shooed 4-year-old Katie and 7-year-old Kevin ahead of her. The children ran through the passageway. And there, at the end, was Mom.

A lump formed in Elsa's throat. I mustn't let myself cry, she told herself. I mustn't.

Mrs. Rose's hair was grayer than Elsa remembered it. Her figure was thicker. Her mouth sagged, and she looked worried. When she saw Elsa and the children, she smiled and rushed towards them.

"Oh, there you are! I was beginning to worry."

Somehow they managed to collect all the suitcases and reach Mrs. Rose's apartment.

* * *

The apartment was big enough for one or two people. Not for five. "I thought you had more room," Elsa said to her mother.

"There's plenty of room. You take the bedroom with Katie and the baby. I borrowed a crib to put in there. And I rented a cot for Kevin. I'll sleep on the couch."

Guilt swept over Elsa. She was 28. Her mother was 56. Twice her age. Her mother had worked hard. And here she was, taking her mother's bed away from her. Elsa was spoiling her mother's chance to rest. I shouldn't have come, Elsa told herself. But just the same, she started unpacking the suitcases. She didn't know what else to do.

Chapter 4

As usual, Elsa couldn't sleep. For months now she had lain awake while others slept. As she lay awake she made plans. Plans to take her own life. Making plans made her feel better.

Elsa needed to feel better. She had a husband and three children to care for. And a house. She had to take care of herself, as well. But how could she take care of anyone or anything when she had no energy? When she couldn't eat? Or sleep? Or make choices?

Bill tried to understand Elsa's sadness. But he couldn't really. He was the kind of person who ate heartily and slept deeply. He was, by nature, optimistic. Elsa just couldn't share his optimism anymore. Nor his humor. Nor his love. And now he had sent her away. It's all my fault, Elsa thought. The sooner I free both of us, the better.

Just before dawn, Elsa fell asleep, exhausted. Shortly after six, Abby woke up. Her cries woke Elsa. I can't, Elsa told herself, I just can't get up. I can't start another stinking day by changing another stinking diaper. "Shut up," she whispered to the baby. Dear God, she thought in despair, have I come to that? Will I hit her next? Abby is such a good baby. She deserves a good mother. But I can't be one. I really can't take care of her. Elsa lay awake praying for the baby to stop crying.

In a few minutes Elsa heard the door open. "Well, hello there," she heard her mother croon to Abby. "How's my baby? You'll come with Grandma, won't you? You and I, we'll have a nice breakfast together. But first we need a dry diaper. That's my girl!" Her mother's voice droned on, calming Abby. Wooing her. Abby was quiet. Finally Elsa heard the door close. She knew her mother had taken the baby.

Now Mom will know what a bad mother I am, Elsa thought. A bad mother is the worst thing a woman can be. But I'm so tired I've just got to sleep. I wish I could close my eyes right now and sleep forever.

Elsa woke at 10:00. Noise from the street came into the apartment. She could hear voices from the apartment above. But her mother's apartment was still. Elsa lay there. Five minutes. Ten minutes. I should get up, she kept telling herself. But her brain wouldn't order her limbs to move.

At last Elsa forced herself off the bed. No one was in the apartment. A magnet held a note to the refrigerator. "Taking children to the beach. Food in the fridge. Have a nice morning."

Have a nice morning! Have a nice morning! The words mocked Elsa. How insane, she thought. As if one person can command another to have a nice morning. Lucky people have nice mornings. Unlucky ones have lousy mornings. But that's Mom. She used to say, "Smile, and the whole world smiles with you. Cry and you cry alone." Now it's "Have a nice morning." She should have my sister Cindy here. Cindy would mind Mom and have a nice morning.

Poor Mom. I'm dumping on her. When I'm gone, the kids will be her responsibility. She'll have to lug the groceries. She'll have to give the baths and change the diapers. She'll have to do the scolding and teaching and jollying along. Elsa looked around the apartment, feeling its emptiness. Hey! I'm alone here. This might be the best time to do it. Right now, before they come back. But do I have enough pills? Maybe Mom has some, she thought, heading for the bathroom.

In the bathroom, Elsa opened the medicine chest. Not much in there. Sunscreen. Ointment good for poison ivy, poison oak, and insect bites. Eyedrops. Mom was never much for pills.

Now, if Dad were the one left behind, his medicine chest would be full of pills. And he would have liquor on hand. Dad understood the magic of pills and liquor. Dad's recipe for life was "Eat what tastes good. Don't move if you don't have to. Drink as much as you can get." In a way, she thought, maybe Dad had killed himself, too.

Well, Elsa decided, pills aren't the only way. Razor blades are useful. A tiny plastic razor lay on the edge of the bathtub. No good. Elsa closed the cabinet and went back into the bedroom. She flopped onto the bed. No ashtray on the nightstand. But she lit a cigarette anyway. The ashes went onto the floor.

It doesn't have to be pills or razor blades. A gun would be faster. Easier. Surer. But where would I get a gun? she asked herself. And I wouldn't know how to load it. And what if one of the kids found me afterwards? No, I couldn't use a gun. Hanging? No, that's not my style. Not jumping out a window, either. An easy way would be carbon monoxide. But for that you have to have a car—your own car.

I could walk out into the ocean, she thought. I could swim out so far I couldn't get back. No. With my luck a shark would take me by the seat of my pants and bring me back to shore. Or the Coast Guard would come after me. Or Mom would rent a rowboat.

Forget it, Elsa told herself. It's not in the cards for today. No, today is not the day. Elsa rose. She looked around for an ashtray. Finding none, she took her cigarette into the kitchen. In her mind she could hear her mother's words, "Elsa, if you have to smoke, at least be careful. You could start a fire."

Fire would do it. But fire is hard to control. You might take others with you. I wouldn't want to do that, Elsa decided. She ran water over the lighted end of the cigarette. Then she flicked the butt into a rubbish can.

There was coffee in a pot on the stove. She found a cup and poured herself some. It was cold and tasted bitter. The cold coffee made her shudder, but she didn't bother to warm it up. She couldn't seem to find the energy to fix something to eat, either. She finally went over to the window and stared out, sipping the cold coffee. After finishing the coffee, she rinsed the cup and went back into the bedroom. She lay down once more.

"Mommy, aren't you dressed yet?" Katie banged the door open.

"I just woke up," Elsa lied.

"We've been to the beach." Kevin threw himself onto the bed. Elsa bounced. "You know what, Mommy?"

"What?"

"Grandma says we can go out to lunch."

Elsa looked at the clock. "You and Grandma go. I'll feed Abby here and put her down for her nap."

Mrs. Rose puffed in. She put Abby into the crib. "My lands, that child weighs more than you do. You should have brought a stroller."

"Hers broke. I'll buy one here. Sorry you had to carry her."

"Don't be sorry. We got along just fine. Now put some clothes on. You're going out for a hamburger."

"No, I can't. Abby naps at one."

"I know that. I said *you* go. Abby and I will eat here."

"I'm not hungry."

"Go anyway. Eat a good lunch. You're just skin and bones, Elsa. I swear I never saw you so thin. You start eating. You hear?"

Mrs. Rose pulled Kevin off the bed. "Come on, children. Wash up while your mother dresses."

Chapter 5

"Wait. Wait at the corner," Elsa screamed at the children.

"Hurry up. You walk so slow, Mommy." Katie pulled on Elsa's arm.

That would be a way, Elsa thought. I could step off the curb. If the light were red, they wouldn't charge the driver. He wouldn't have to suffer. But maybe he would, anyway. No, I mustn't involve other people. And not with the kids along. They'd never forget it. They'd have nightmares.

"Mommy?"

"Yes, Katie?"

"Mommy, I don't want a hamburger. Do I have to have a hamburger, Mommy?"

"No. Have what you want."

"But I don't know what I want. What do I want, Mommy?"

"We'll see." Elsa glanced into the street. Oh, my God! There was Don, driving very slowly, looking all over for her. "Here," Elsa called to the children. "We're going to turn here. At this corner."

"No, Mommy. We're at the restaurant," Kevin said. "See? It says Best Burgers In Town on the window. Grandma said we'd know it if it said that. I read it, Mommy, all by myself."

"Turn anyway. Just for a minute. Please, Kevin."

"Why, Mommy?"

Too late. The car slid to the curb. "Elsa?"

Elsa stared straight ahead. Maybe if she did not look at him, Don would evaporate.

"Elsa, I have to talk to you."

"Not now. Not here."

"When? Where?"

"Please, just go away and leave me alone."

"Me and Mommy and Kevin, we're going to eat lunch in this store," Katie confided to Don.

"Thank you, sweetheart. I'll come in, too, and buy you a chocolate sundae."

Don slowly moved his car towards the parking lot entrance.

"Look, Kevin, there's another hamburger place across the street. That one looks better. Let's go there." Elsa tried to grasp each child by a hand.

"No. Grandma said the hamburgers are best here."

"Katie doesn't even want a burger."

"But *I* do, Mommy!" Kevin said. "I'm tired of walking and I'm hungry!"

Kevin made it plain that wild horses could not pull him away from that restaurant.

They entered. Elsa could not concentrate on the menu. She kept glancing at the door.

"What can I have?" Katie whined.

"Do you want a cheese sandwich?"

"Unh-uh, I don't want any sandwich."

"How about a bowl of chicken noodle soup? You like that."

"No, I don't. I want crackers in milk."

"Aw, Katie. You don't eat that in a restaurant," Kevin scolded her. "You eat things you can't get at home."

"Is that right, Mommy? Do I have to eat something I don't eat at home?"

"No, if you want crackers in milk, that's what I'll order for you."

"See," Katie said, sticking her tongue out at Kevin. "Look, Mommy. There's that man. He's going to buy me a chocolate someday. What's a *chocolate someday*, Mommy?"

Though she didn't want to, Elsa looked toward the door. Don caught her eye. He came over and sat down at her table.

"What's a chocolate someday?" Katie asked him.

"I'll get you one. Then you'll see. You, too," he told Kevin.

"I already know what it is."

"I'll get you one anyway. Listen, kids, I want to talk to your mommy. I'm going to take your mommy to another table while you sit here. OK?"

"No. Mommy has to break my crackers."

"I'm staying right here," Elsa told Don. "I'm eating with my children. You're way out of line."

"*I'm* out of line! *I'm* out of line! Listen, I leave my family. I leave my job. I drive all night. I go without sleep. I don't know what the hell is going on with you! When I finally do catch up with you, you tell me I'm out of line. That's a laugh!"

"Keep your voice down. How did you find me?"

"I went to your mom's place. She said you weren't there. But she was holding the baby, so I figured you hadn't gone far."

"Mommy, I'm hungry. Where's my hamburger?"

"Don, make yourself useful. Find a waitress."

"They take orders at the counter. What do you want?"

"A hamburger, plain, for Kevin. Crackers and milk for Katie. Coffee for me."

"I want a milk shake with my hamburger," Kevin insisted.

"OK. And I'm going to bring a shake for your mother instead of coffee."

"No, Don, that's too rich."

"Drink it. You're going to starve yourself to death one of these days, Elsa."

"I eat," Elsa said.

"Like hell you do," Don said.

"Please don't swear in front of the children."

"Does your father ever say hell?" Don asked Kevin and Katie.

"Sometimes," Kevin said. "Mommy tells him not to."

"Your mommy's good at telling people not to." Don rose and went to the counter.

"Who is that man?" Kevin asked his mother.

"Someone I know. You don't know him."

"Does Daddy?"

"No."

"Why does he want to buy us stuff?" Kevin asked.

Elsa looked at him a moment before answering. "Because he's a friend of mine," she said.

"You don't act like he's a friend. You act like you wish he'd go away."

"I do wish he'd go away. He used to be a friend. He's not anymore."

"What's he mad at you about?"

"Kevin, you don't have to know everything. You ask too many questions."

"*I* don't. Do I, Mommy? I don't ask too many questions." Katie stood on her chair and put her face into Elsa's.

"Sit down, Katie." How many times a day do I tell that child to sit down? Elsa asked

herself. Of the three children, she annoys me the most. Yet I feel closest to her. She's like me. I dread watching her grow up. She'll hurt and be hurt. Abby is just like Bill. She'll love everybody. Kevin will push himself where he wants to go. But Katie.... Elsa put her hand over Katie's and squeezed.

Don returned, carrying their order. He had indeed brought a milk shake for Elsa. Elsa stirred it, round and round, with a straw.

"When can I see you?" Don asked.

"I don't know," Elsa answered.

"Where's my chocolate someday?" Katie demanded.

"I'll get it." Don brought the sundaes to the table. "Here."

"That's just ice cream with chocolate sauce," Katie complained.

"Life, my dear young lady," Don said, "is a series of disappointments. Nothing is as good as it sounds. Get used to the idea."

"Say thank you," Elsa prompted.

"But, Mommy, it's just ice cream with chocolate sauce," Katie complained.

"Say thank you anyway."

"When can I see you?" Don asked, leaning over the table towards Elsa.

"Will you give me a drink? A real one?" Elsa asked him.

"If that's what it takes," he answered.

"I need a drink," Elsa told him. "My mom hates the stuff. She thinks it killed my dad. There's no liquor at all in her apartment."

"I'm staying at a friend's condo. He's out of town. I'll pick you up at nine."

"Make it ten. But I'm not promising!"

"I have a surprise for you."

A faint smile showed on Elsa's face. The smile was not because of Don's surprise. She smiled because an idea had just occurred to her.

* * *

"You'll never guess who was here looking for you," Mrs. Rose greeted Elsa.

"Don Gibbons. I know because he found me."

"Have you taken up with him again, Elsa? I can't imagine why you would."

"Mommy's going to his condo tonight," Kevin broke in. "What's a condo, Grandma?"

"It's like an apartment. I doubt your mother will go there."

"I may," Elsa said. "I may not."

Chapter 6

"Why, Elsa? Why? That's all I want to know," Mrs. Rose asked softly. Kevin was asleep on his cot nearby.

"Why what?"

"Why are you cheating on Bill?"

"I'm not. That's all over. I didn't want Don to follow me here. That was his idea." Elsa pulled on her cigarette. She was lying on the couch. Her mother stood looking down on her. Elsa turned her head away. She couldn't bear to meet her mother's eyes.

Mrs. Rose pushed Elsa's legs back and sat on the edge of the couch. "Are you unhappy with Bill, dear?"

Smoke made Elsa's eyes water. "I suppose so," she said.

"What happened? You two were so much in love."

"Nothing happened. It's not Bill's fault. He tried to be nice."

"But what about Bill, Elsa? Are you planning to leave him?"

Elsa tried to laugh the question off. Instead, she choked on the smoke from her cigarette. She began to cough and couldn't stop. Her chest hurt. She sat up and snuffed out the cigarette in an ashtray on the coffee table.

Her mother went to the kitchen, got a glass of water, and handed it to Elsa. She drank it. As she handed the glass back to her mother, she looked into Mrs. Rose's face. The concern she saw there made her feel ashamed. She cleared her throat. "Don't worry about me, Mom. I'm going to be all right. Soon everything will be all right."

"Are you in love with Don, Elsa?"

"No, Mom. I never was."

"Then why go with him tonight?"

"I have personal reasons—reasons I can't talk about."

"Does Bill know about Don?"

"I don't think so. Bill is too wrapped up in the gas station. He isn't home enough to notice things."

"Well, of course, whenever a person goes into business.... But, to get back to Don, Elsa—"

"Stop pressing me, will you please, Mom?" Elsa's voice was sharp. "That's what Bill does. He keeps asking questions. He looks at me as if he can see my insides. I can't stand someone prying. Leave me alone, Mom."

"Bill's your husband. He has a right to ask questions."

"Believe me, I'm not blaming Bill. Not one bit. Bill's had it tough. I'm not easy to live with. You know that, Mom."

"I know nothing of the sort. What makes you say that?"

Elsa lit another cigarette. She took several puffs before she answered. "Cindy was the daughter you loved best, Mom. No matter how hard I tried, you always loved Cindy better."

"Elsa! That just isn't so. Cindy was a cheerful soul. She took whatever came. You were always sensitive, like your father. I loved him, too, Elsa. No matter what you think, I loved you and your dad as much as I loved Cindy."

"You gave her a cute name."

"Why, Elsa. You know very well I gave you my grandmother's name. I loved that woman. I loved her name, too. *Cindy* was just a name I picked out of the blue."

"Remember the time...." Elsa began to weep.

"Remember what time, honey?"

"We were both sick. Cindy and I had chicken pox or something. We both called

31

you. You went to Cindy first." Sobs overcame Elsa.

"I can't believe that hurt you. One of you had to be first. You remind me of that old joke, Elsa. A mother gave her son two neckties. One was red, one was blue. The next morning, he came downstairs wearing the blue one. 'What's the matter?' she shrieked. 'You don't like the red one?'"

Elsa gave a weak smile. Then she cried harder.

"Honey, are you sick? You don't act at all well."

"I knew you'd say that. Mom, I've gone to scads of doctors. They all say the same thing."

"What's that?"

"They tell me to go to a psychiatrist. In other words, they think it's all in my head. They think I'm nuts. Do you think I'm nuts, Mom? Tell the truth."

"I think a girl as unhappy and run-down as you may need a psychiatrist. I'm not saying you're insane, I'm just saying—"

Elsa stood up. "I've gotta get dressed." She went into the bathroom and closed the door behind her. In the bathroom, she stood for a minute with her head and buttocks pressed against the closed door. Tears ran down her face. "A girl as unhappy and run-down as you...." That's double-talk for "a girl as sick and crazy as you," she thought. How did Bill put it? "When I see my pretty little wife lying around and crying...." His pretty little wife indeed! He only married me because I was pregnant with Kevin. I should have refused to marry him. I should have raised Kevin by myself. It was my mistake.

Why can't I do it and get it over with? Elsa asked herself. Why didn't I bring more pills? I should have gone to a new doctor for more sleeping pills. I could have begged pills from friends. I could have asked each of them to lend me a couple of barbs. Just to tide me over until I could see a doctor in Florida. If each of them had given me just a few.... Well, I didn't do that. I'd better be sure to take every single one with me tonight. Elsa blew her nose.

Elsa's cosmetic bag sat on the bathroom windowsill. Out of it she took a tin box that had once held small bandages. She opened the box and stirred her finger through beige capsules, white discs, blue triangles. Over the bottom of the basin she spread a dry washcloth. One by one, she took the pills from the box and counted them onto the cloth. "Fifty-three," she said out loud as she put down the last one. I wonder if that's enough, she thought.

What if I take them and they're not enough? But if I drink a lot, I won't need so many. Bill taught me that. He yelled at me when he caught me taking pills and drinking. "If you take all those pills, kid, you can't drink like that! You'll kill yourself that way."

Elsa took up the tin box once more. Into it, one by one, she put the capsules. Then the discs. The triangles went on top. Gently she closed the hinged lid, took the box, and put it into her purse.

"I guess I'm ready," she said as she walked out of the bathroom.

"I thought you were going to change your clothes."

Elsa looked down at herself and saw peach stains on her T-shirt. Her jeans were as old as Katie. They'd gotten too big now, and bagged at the knees and seat. Ankle socks and old gym shoes completed her costume. "I'm too tired to change," she said.

"It's no skin off my nose," Mrs. Rose muttered. "What time is he coming?"

"Ten o'clock."

"Well, it's only nine. Sit down and have a cup of tea."

Uh-oh, Elsa thought. What she really wants is for me to sit down while she tries to straighten me out.

"I think I'll change after all," she said.

In the bedroom, Elsa stared into the closet. All the clothes seemed to look alike. She touched each one. This? No. This? No. How does one choose, she wondered. What difference does it make what I wear? Then she thought of what was going to happen later. I want to have on something decent when they lay me out, she thought. She pulled out a yellow dress with a wide skirt. Bill had always liked that on her. She found stockings and high-heeled shoes, clean underwear, and a slip. I haven't dressed up this much in years, she told herself. Or is it only months? It's getting hard to keep track of time.

After a bath, she carefully put on makeup. I'm glad, she told herself, I'm glad I've finally made a decision. I know where and when and how. When she left the bathroom, she felt pretty good.

"Well, that's more like it," her mother said. "Though I wish it were Bill coming for you. You look pretty."

"Thank you. If you don't mind, I'll wait outside."

"Just as you please."

"I mean, Kevin is asleep in the front room. And you may want to undress."

"Elsa?"

"Yes?"

"I hope this is the end of your seeing Don Gibbons. Please send him packing for good."

"Don't worry. I will." Elsa came close to Mrs. Rose. "Mom, thanks for everything. I'm glad you get along so well with the children. They can learn a lot from you." She put her arms around her mother.

Mrs. Rose seemed a little embarrassed. But she hugged back and kissed Elsa's cheek. "You've always been a good girl. Stay that way, honey."

"It's too late to tell me that, Mom. Good-bye."

"Good-bye, dear. Have a good time."

From the worried look on Mrs. Rose's face, Elsa guessed her mother wished her a good time only out of habit.

Chapter 7

Elsa sat in a deep chair in the shiny, modern, condominium. She seemed to be listening to Don. What she was really listening to were her own thoughts. Inside she felt calm. In command of herself. Better than she had felt for several months.

I'm going to do it, she told herself. At last I have a foolproof plan. I'll drink myself silly. Don will do the same. He always passes out after a few drinks. I'll wash the pills down with the rest of the whiskey. Then I'll sit in this chair. This is where they'll find me in the morning.

I can hear them now. Mom'll say, "Surely, she didn't mean to do it." But Bill will know better. He'll say, "I knew this would happen one day. Elsa drank like a fish. She also took sleeping pills and tranquilizers."

Don will sputter around. "I hadn't seen her in years," he'll say. "We just ran into each other recently, here in Florida."

Everyone will lie to the children. They'll say I had a heart attack or a brain tumor or something. And poor Mom. She's going to get stuck with the kids. But she'll sort of understand. She'll make the best of it the way she always does. And I'll be gone. Done for. Departed. What a relief.

"Don," Elsa said, "I'll have more of the same."

Don filled Elsa's glass, but not his own. "As I was saying, Elsa, I finally decided to leave Amy. I'll ask her for a divorce when I get back. It's going to take her a while to get used to the idea. But she'll come around. In some ways, Amy's a good sport."

With some difficulty, Elsa rose from her chair. She nudged Don's knee with her own. "Dance with me," she commanded.

"Now? My leaving Amy is the surprise I was talking about. If we're both divorced—"

"What you and Amy do is your business. I'm not divorcing Bill. Come on. Let's dance."

When Don didn't get up, Elsa started to dance by herself. She put one of her arms across her body and held the other in the air. She hummed a tune as she rocked her hips and stepped in a circle.

Don stared at her in disbelief. "Elsa, don't you understand? This is our chance for happiness together."

"I'm happy. I'm happier now than I've been in ages. Let Amy be happy, too. If she doesn't leave you, you shouldn't leave her. Amy's a good sport. You said so yourself." Elsa laughed to herself for a minute. Then she stopped dancing, rubbed her right forefinger over her left, and recited in a childish voice, "Shamey, shamey, you're leaving Amy. If I'm to blamey, then shamey me."

For a minute Elsa resumed dancing. Then she stopped again and began to laugh. She laughed so hard she doubled over.

"What's the joke?"

"I'm the joke. I'm funny, aren't I, Donald, old boy? A barrel of laughs. That's me, Elsa Rose Caukins. A riot. A comedienne. A wit. A..."

"A drunk. That's what you are. If you could see yourself—" Don pushed himself out of his chair. He put his hands roughly on Elsa's shoulders. "I should wring your neck! Playing games with me! Leading me on!"

Elsa shrugged out of his grasp, picked up her glass and drained it. "Another, please, bartender. Make this one bigger. You were stingy with the last one."

"The bar's closed. I'll take you home."

"No, I want to stay. I need another drink."

"You need something, Elsa. But it's not another drink. You were never in love with me. Were you, Elsa?"

"I never said I was."

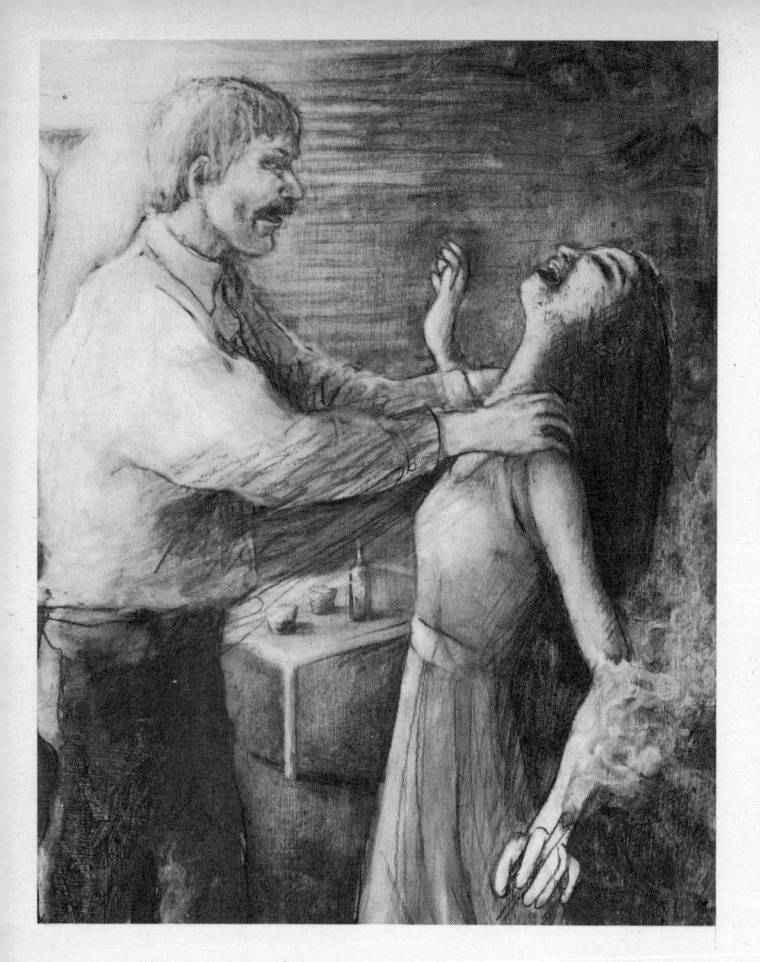

"Then why did you come on so strong?"

"I was drowning. Drowning people clutch at straws. For a while, you were the best straw—a dancing, drinking, handsome straw. But now I'm doing away with straws. If I drown, I drown. As of tonight I don't need you anymore. Dance with me, Don. Pour me another drink. Then let's tango. Isn't that a movie or something? *The Last Tango*?"

"The way I heard it, it takes two to tango. I must have been crazy to get mixed up with you. You've been cheating on me as much as you have on Bill. Come on. I'm taking you home."

"No, I want to stay here."

"I said, come on! I'll have to drive all night and all day tomorrow as it is. Amy's going to have a fit. But she'll calm down. Boy, I thought Amy was a tough customer. Compared to you, she's easy. Now, come on! Right now!" Don grabbed Elsa's shoulder roughly and propelled her out the door.

* * *

Mrs. Rose was still awake when Elsa came in. "Well, that was quick. Did you give him his walking papers?"

"Yes."

"Good. Elsa, I've been thinking. I have the most wonderful idea. Elsa, how would you like—"

"Not now, Mom. Tell me in the morning."

* * *

Elsa lay on her back, legs straight out, arms at her sides. I loused it up again, she thought. I'm such a fool. Even a lightweight like Don has more integrity than I do. He's sincere. I'm not. He's capable of loving. I'm not. He's sane. I'm crazy.

I was going to use him tonight. Set him up so his wife would know he'd been unfaithful. I would have hurt him, too. Ruined his life in a way. I keep telling myself I don't want to hurt people. Yet I hurt people all the time.

There's too much hurting in the world, she thought. Scenes came into Elsa's mind. Babies starving in Africa. Asian boat people being turned back to sea. Refugees in barren camps. Warring troops wiping out whole villages. People being tortured. People being neglected. One after another, horrors paraded through her brain. She felt the suffering of the whole world. How can people bear to live? she wondered.

Why should I let myself live? Good, decent folk, through no fault of their own, suffer and die. I'm not worth the space I take up. The food I eat. Some people help others. I make life hard for everyone I touch. The world will be a better place without me.

Chapter 8

Again Mrs. Rose took care of Abby in the morning.

Elsa was awake, but she pretended to sleep. She thought about how her life would seem to someone else. She lay on clean sheets in a cheerful room. Good food was hers if she opened the door. Her husband made a decent living. Her children were healthy. Her mother was kind. Two men said they loved her. Yet she felt a sense of doom. Nothing seemed right in her life. And things were getting worse.

* * *

"Let me tell you what I have in mind," Mrs. Rose sang out as she set Abby into her crib. Abby, fed and changed, was content. "How would you like to go to Nassau?"

"I don't know. I never thought about it."

"Well, they have boats going every day. They leave at night. You spend a couple of days there. The boat is your hotel in port. It's supposed to be a lovely trip. How would you like to go?"

"I don't think so. Besides, I can't afford it."

"I'll give you the trip as a gift."

"You can't afford it, either."

"Never mind. I'll manage. It will be good for you, Elsa. You'll get away from the kids. You'll rest. The salt water will give you an appetite. The food is supposed to be luscious. It might be just what the doctor ordered."

"It's too much trouble. I'd have to pack."

"You packed to come here—much more than you'll need there."

"Bill packed. I couldn't. Taking a trip is too much hassle, Mom. Thanks anyway."

"Think about it," Mrs. Rose coaxed. "We have to buy a stroller today. Let's stop at a travel agency while we're out."

Elsa imagined herself on a ship. The other passengers were asleep in their rooms. Only she was on deck. She stood at the stern, watching the wake. Then she stepped onto a bench. From there, she climbed onto the rail. And then she dived into the water. The taste of salt water came into her mouth. Cold enveloped her head and body. She dropped down, down, down. She relaxed and let herself go. She did nothing to make herself rise again.

No one would miss her until the next day. Or until the ship docked back in Miami.

"All right," she said. "Maybe I will go."

Chapter 9

Mrs. Rose bought the cheapest ticket. That meant Elsa shared a tiny stateroom with three other women. Two of them were traveling together. They pretended they were in a room of their own. They took possession of one set of bunks. They talked only to each other.

That was fine with Elsa. However, the third roommate, Claire, assumed she was paired with Elsa. To Claire, this trip to Nassau was as thrilling as being shot to the moon. She expected Elsa to share her excitement. "Imagine," Claire gushed, "we're crossing the Atlantic Ocean! Tomorrow we'll see a foreign country! With a different flag! And different money! And different customs! Couldn't you just die!"

"Yes," Elsa answered. "I could."

After dinner, Claire clutched Elsa's arm. "Let's go to the bar. Liquor is cheap on board ship because there's no tax. Besides, there may be some cute guys in the bar."

There were several cute guys in the bar. But they were all with cute girls. Claire was right on one score. Liquor was cheap. Elsa drank a lot. Claire chattered without stopping. Every once in a while Elsa said, "I see."

"Let's not go to bed tonight," Claire suggested as they left the bar. "I don't want to miss one minute of the trip."

Towards midnight, the two women took blankets from their bunks. Out on deck, they found chairs, took off their shoes, and snuggled the blankets around themselves. "Isn't this great!" Claire raved.

The moon threw a streak of light onto the calm sea. A slight breeze brought the fresh smell of salt water. This is perfect, Elsa thought. When she dived into the ocean she would return to nature. No remains. No funeral. No grave.

Elsa relaxed, lit a cigarette, and just let her mind wander. Whenever she drank a lot she couldn't focus her thoughts for long. That, she felt, was a blessing. Claire talked, but Elsa did not listen. After a while, Claire tired of talking and dozed off. A couple walked by. No one else was in sight.

Elsa pushed her blanket off and put her shoes on. Carefully she stood up, swaying a little. This would be her first chance to examine the rail. Heavens, it was high. And the sides were slick and solid. No place to gain a foothold. Besides, the rail was recessed from the deck's edge. It would be impossible to dive from the rail. She would have to go over the rail and jump from the edge.

Footsteps. A man passed her. Then he came back. "See the phosphorescence?" he asked.

"See the what?"

"Phosphorescence. Light in the water. Watch."

He took a coin from his pocket and threw it into the water. "See? Pretty, isn't it?"

"Very pretty." Elsa had seen no lights. She suspected the man was as drunk as she. Probably trying to pick her up. "I'm waiting for my husband," she said. "He won't like your talking to me."

The man made a sort of lazy salute and left.

If only there was something to give me a boost, Elsa thought. The deck chair? No. It would make noise and maybe wake Claire. She paced along the rail for a while. Aha! A container of life jackets. Sort of far from the rail, though. Could she make it?

The top of the container was rounded and slippery. Elsa climbed onto it using her hands and knees. Slowly she rose to her feet and took a few baby steps toward the rail. A short leap and she was pulling her body onto the rail as a swimmer would climb out of a pool.

Did she feel the hand before she heard the voice? Or did the voice sound before the hand grasped? "Good morning," the voice said. "Up sort of early, aren't you?" The man's face was so close to hers Elsa could see the little wrinkles around his eyes. "Let me help you down," he said. "We don't like passengers to go beyond the rail. Too easy to slip, you know."

He was a large, middle-aged man, wearing the cap and insignia of a ship's officer. His hand went completely around Elsa's upper arm. He helped her down to the deck as gently as he could. "You don't want to do that, miss," he said.

"Yes, I do. Please let go of my arm." Elsa began to weep.

The officer wrapped his big arms around her. "If you need a shoulder to cry on, mine might do."

As Elsa cried, the man talked. "You're not the first one. It's gotten so we have to patrol the decks at night. I guess maybe if I were that unhappy, I'd do the same. Nothing so clean as the ocean. Nothing so close to God. But you don't have to rush things, you know. If God wants you, miss, He'll call you soon enough."

Elsa pushed herself loose. "Thank you," she said. "I'll be all right now."

"Oh, I'm not in a hurry. Come on, sit down for a while." He led her to a bench.

"You know, I don't pretend to understand," the man said. "The people who try to do it are ordinary people. When they come on board, no one could pick them out—the ones who are going to try it, I mean. You never know who's wearing a mask. Who's smiling on the outside, but crying on the inside. You never know who's going to try to slip over the side.

"Take you, for instance. A pretty girl like you. I bet you have a nice family. I bet you have a lot to live for. Why can't you say to yourself, 'I'm going to buck up and be happy?'"

"I don't know why. I just can't."

"A wonderful night like this. With so much beauty, how can you feel so desperate?"

Elsa sniffed. Her voice shook. "Beauty makes it worse. It's the contrast, see? When you're all rotten inside you can't stand sharing a beautiful world with good people."

"Nobody's all rotten. Nobody's all good. We're all equal in the sight of God."

"That's your opinion." Sobs shook Elsa once more. "Please," she said. "Let me do it. It's getting light. This is my last chance."

"Elsa." It was Claire. "I looked all over for you. I was beginning to think you'd fallen in." Claire laughed. "Oh, listen, dear, I didn't mean to interrupt. I'm sorry. Just so you're all right."

"Do you share a cabin with this lady?" the man asked Claire.

"Yes, why?"

"Would you take her to your stateroom? I think she's overtired. She ought to rest."

"Sure," Claire said. "Come on, Elsa. Let's sleep."

"So long, Elsa," the man said. "My name is Jack. I'll look you up later."

Out of earshot, Claire exclaimed, "Oh boy. Can you ever pick 'em! Does he have a friend?"

"It's not what you think."

"Hey! Have you been crying? You look as if you've been crying."

"Yes, I don't feel well. If you don't mind, Claire, I'd rather not talk."

* * *

Jack went ashore with Claire and Elsa. He showed them the straw market. He took them into shops. He showed them court in session where the lawyers and judge were wearing white wigs. Then he led them into a church. He told them the story of how the church came to be. As they left, he whispered to Elsa, "I thought you might want to pray." He doesn't understand, Elsa thought. He's in touch with God. I'm not. I don't know how to pray anymore. I don't know what to pray *for*.

Nassau bored Elsa. She wanted the tour to end. She wanted everything to end. She didn't want to have to see anything. She didn't want to hear. She didn't want to feel the motion of her legs. She didn't want to be.

She knew Jack was trying to be nice. To be helpful. But she felt he was watching her. It reminded her of a joke. A very pregnant woman hails a cab. "Where to, lady?" the cabbie asks. "City Hospital," the woman replies. "Not in my cab," the departing cabbie yells. Jack is telling me, "Not on my ship, lady." I'll bet he's going to watch me till I get home.

Claire was delighted with every new thing Jack showed them. She laughed gaily at the things he said. After a while, Jack paid more attention to her than to Elsa. Elsa was glad.

Sure enough, when they put into Miami, Jack came to their room. "I have a car. I'll take you home," he told Claire and Elsa.

Claire beamed. "Why, thank you." As soon as she closed the door, she chirped, "Isn't he the nicest man?" Then she remembered. "He'll drop me off first, of course. You're the one who found him."

"He's all yours," Elsa said. "I'm married."

When Jack dropped Elsa at her door, he seemed glad to be rid of her.

Chapter 10

"Well, how was your trip?" Mrs. Rose asked Elsa.

"Nice. Thank you for sending me."

"I hope you feel better. Elsa, must you light a cigarette the moment you walk in the house? You smoke too much. What did you buy?" she asked, turning her attention to Elsa's shopping bag.

Elsa opened the bag so her mother could see the bottles of liquor.

"You know I don't like that stuff in my house."

"It was such a bargain, I couldn't resist."

"Grandma, look what I drew." Katie burst in. She stuck a piece of paper in front of Mrs. Rose's eyes.

"What is it, dear?"

"I don't know. What is it, Grandma?"

"Well, whatever it is, it's very pretty. You haven't told your mother hello yet."

"Hello," Katie said. "Grandma, are you going to take us to the park like you said?"

"Not today, honey. Today your mommy will take care of you. Mrs. Moore, upstairs, is having a card party. She asked me to come. Is that all right with you, Elsa?"

I've been gone just two days, Elsa thought. In two days my mother has become my children's mother. I'm the sitter. That's what I wanted, I suppose. That's why I brought them here. Just the same, it hurts. Out loud, she said, "You don't have to ask me, Mother. Go out whenever you want."

Elsa went into the bedroom and closed the door. Abby would probably sleep for about two hours. That should be time enough. She took the bottle of Scotch from its bag, uncorked it, and took a long swallow. That's for openers, she thought. She put the tin box, full of pills, on the nightstand.

No note, she decided for the hundredth time. Let them always think it was just an accident. One more drink from the bottle. Then back to the front room. "Go ahead, Mom. Enjoy yourself."

"Kevin, Katie, come upstairs with me. I want you to see where I'll be." Mrs. Rose whispered to Elsa, "I want to show them off to the women."

She's afraid there'll be trouble, Elsa thought. She wants them to know where to get her. She doesn't trust me to take care of them. Perhaps I should be thankful she's taken over so easily.

Kevin and Katie came back in a few minutes. Elsa met them at the door. "I think I'll lie down for a nap. Would you two like to play outside?"

"No. Hey! I've got an idea. Katie, let's draw pictures for Grandma. Let's put them all around. When she comes back we'll yell, 'Surprise!'"

"Yes, let's do that." Katie knelt on a chair. She grabbed paper and crayons and started drawing.

"You draw for the kitchen. I'll draw for the front room," Kevin ordered.

"No. *You* draw for the kitchen. *I'll* draw for the front room."

They don't give a damn about me, Elsa thought, pitying herself. As she went through the bedroom doorway, she tripped and fell against the baby's crib. It shook and rattled. The slats made a loud noise. Frightened, Abby woke up, crying. She raised her arms to her mother.

"I'm sorry," Elsa told her. She picked up the baby, hugged and kissed her. "You represent all the good, innocent people on earth. I beg your pardon. Pardon me for living." Will that be my last act on earth, she wondered. To apologize to a baby?

Elsa carried Abby into the front room and placed her on the floor. "Let her crawl around a bit," she told Kevin and Katie. "But watch her. Don't let her get into Grandma's things."

"You look tired, Mommy," Kevin said. "Maybe you better take a nap. We'll watch Abby."

"Thank you. You're a good boy." Elsa kissed Kevin's cheek. Then Katie's.

"Ugh." Katie drew away. "You smell bad again." She wiped Elsa's kiss from her face.

"I'm sorry," Elsa mumbled as she lurched into the bedroom and closed the door behind her. Sitting on the edge of the bed, she took the tin box from the nightstand and opened it. There were the little blue triangles on top.

How shall I take them? she asked herself. One by one will take too long. Maybe by threes or fours. She counted out four triangles and shoved them into her mouth. Then she took a swig of whiskey. The pills went down. Another four. Another and another. Now, she was into the white discs. They were harder to swallow. She choked and sputtered.

Elsa reached toward the nightstand for a tissue. The whole box of tissues came forward, knocking the tin box off the nightstand. Pills spilled onto the floor and scattered in all directions. "Oh, no," Elsa

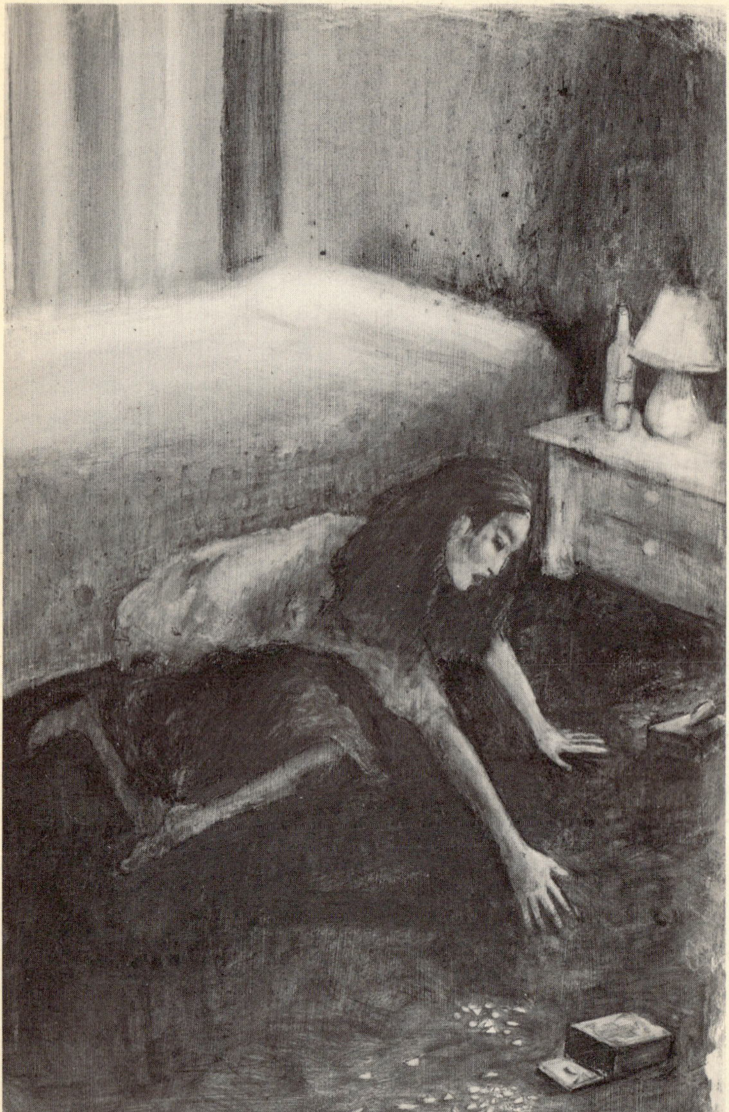

moaned. "I don't have enough as it is." She wiped her mouth on the tissue.

Dizzy and weak, Elsa slid from the bed to the floor. She could see the pills scattered about. But, somehow, she didn't know where to begin picking them up. "Blind drunk," she said out loud. "That's what I am, blind drunk." She picked up a capsule and put it into her mouth. She needed whiskey to wash it down. But the whiskey was on the nightstand. With elbows on the bed, she tried to raise herself. But her feet kept slipping out from under her. She could feel them pushing the pills farther and farther away.

A loud knock sounded on the door.

"Mommmeee!" Kevin screamed.

"What do you want?"

"It's Abby. She found a box under the sink. I think she ate from it. Mommy, it has the skeleton head on it."

Elsa tried to rise from the floor. She couldn't make it. "Get Grandma!" she yelled as loud as she could. Then she passed out.

Chapter 11

Elsa remained unconscious during the ambulance ride. She was not aware when doctors pumped the drugs and alcohol from her stomach.

The next day she awoke. "Where am I?" she asked the woman in the next bed.

"In the hospital. You made an attempt, didn't you?"

Oh, my God, Elsa thought. I tried and it didn't work. I failed at that, too. She closed her eyes. Suddenly, a strange voice startled her.

"Mrs. Caukins?" Elsa's eyes flew open. "You're awake, are you? Fine. I'm Doctor Collins. You'll find your clothes in the closet over there. Dress and come out to the sun room. End of the hall to your right."

Dr. Collins was reading Elsa's chart as she entered the sun room. He was a young man. Not much older than Elsa. "Now, let's see," he said. "You are a little thing. Don't weigh much. We don't want to overdose you. Yet... I'll tell you what. I'm going to start you on a fairly stiff dose of something that will help you feel less depressed. If you have trouble, tell the doctors here."

"Aren't you a doctor?"

"Yes, but not on this staff. They just let me come in to see you. You're in a general hospital, Elsa. For the next week or ten days, you'll stay here. You'll take tests. They want to see that the overdose didn't do great harm."

"What—what harm could it do?"

"Don't worry about it. They just have to make sure. After they're sure, you'll come to my place."

"I don't understand. If I'm all right, I'll go home."

"No, Elsa, we have to treat your depression. I have offices at a psychiatric hospital. Do you know what that means?"

"Yes. It's a hospital for crazy people."

"Some people would say that. A person who tries to kill herself is depressed, Elsa. Depression is a kind of mental illness. A curable illness. You don't have to stay depressed."

"Who brought you into this?"

"As I heard the story, your mother telephoned your husband. You live in the north somewhere?"

"Yes."

"Your husband called your doctor there. That doctor called my hospital. And, well, here I am."

An old feeling came to Elsa. She was sitting in the office of the doctor at home. He was pushing her to see a psychiatrist. "Oh, that old quack! Can't I decide anything for myself?"

Dr. Collins leaned forward. "That's what it's all about, Elsa. I'll do my damnedest to give you back to yourself. As fast as possible. That's why I came right away. The sooner you start the medicine.... It should begin to work in a couple of weeks."

"A couple of weeks?"

"Yes. These medicines are slow. Besides that, they don't always work. We may have to start over with something else."

"What do you mean 'work'?"

"Lift you out of your depression. That's why you tried to kill yourself, isn't it? Because you couldn't stand your depression?"

"No, because I couldn't stand me."

"What do you mean?"

Elsa was going to say, "I don't know," but Dr. Collins looked so interested, she tried to answer.

"Well," she said, "depression is feeling sad. I've felt sad lots of times. In high school I flunked French. I worked and I worked. I tried and I tried. But I flunked. And I thought, 'I'm dumb. My best isn't good enough.' So I was depressed about it. But I didn't feel the way I feel now. In the back of my mind, I knew I'd be all right pretty soon.

"I feel different now. I wish I could describe what goes on in my head. Did you ever, maybe, all of a sudden, ask yourself, 'Who am I?' I mean did you ask yourself in a scary way? In a way you couldn't answer with your name or by describing yourself?"

"Yeah. I think I know what you mean. You ask yourself, 'What is this being called *me*? Why am I here? At this time? In this place? With this name?' You question your right to be alive. Religious people might say you come face to face with your soul. Yep. That is scary."

"That's sort of how I feel. All the time. Hidden, secret parts of me have taken over my brain. I can't keep my mind on anything outside myself. I can't turn myself off by working or sleeping or laughing or reading or making love. I'm so full of myself, I can't do anything for anybody. I'm scared silly all the time. Of everything. Of everybody."

"We have different words for the different kinds of depression," Dr. Collins said. "You're right. There is ordinary depression like that you felt when you flunked French. Clinical depression—like you have now—is different. And worse."

"I hurt people."

"You saved your baby's life. Or at least you thought you did. You gave up your chance to end your agony in order to save her."

A memory stabbed Elsa. "Oh, God!" she cried out, remembering. "What about Abby? What happened to her?"

"She's quite all right. She may or may not have put the poison into her mouth. Did you know that your little girl...I forget her name..."

"Katie?"

"Yes, Katie. Katie wiped the baby's mouth out. She took a paper napkin. Your mother found her doing it when she came in. That was the smartest thing anyone could have done. Nothing was in the baby's stomach when they pumped it. No poison, I mean."

"Katie's very bright, Doctor. But I'm not good for her. She gets under my skin. I'm not good for the others, either."

"'The others' meaning...?"

"The baby, my little boy, my husband. I'm an awful wife, Doctor Collins. I've done awful things to Bill. I've—I've even been unfaithful."

Before she knew it, Elsa was telling Dr. Collins about Don. She told him the truth. Telling it made her cry. But she felt good to be telling it at last.

Chapter 12

Ten days later, Elsa moved into the psychiatric hospital.

"I don't want you to just lie around," Dr. Collins told her. "Keep up and move around. Once we know the medicine is working, you can go home."

"No hurry," Elsa said.

I'm supposed to hate this, she thought. I'm locked up in a booby bin. Society doesn't trust me to take care of myself. I haven't trusted myself in a long time. In a way, it's good to be somebody else's problem. She said as much to Dr. Collins. He smiled. "When you begin screaming to get out, I'll know you're better," he said.

The medicine made Elsa groggy. Being groggy took the edge off her mental pain. She slept more. She ate more. She talked to other people on the ward. "You said it would take two weeks," she told Dr. Collins. "I feel better already."

"If we took you off the medicine, you'd drift back to where you were. I meant two weeks for a real start towards recovery. You're not having any side effects, are you?"

"None that bother me much."

"Does your mother come to see you?"

Elsa lit a cigarette before she answered. "No. I talk to my mother on the telephone. I'd feel guilty if she came here in all this heat. I tell her not to come. It's bad enough I've saddled her with the children."

"Do you talk to the children, too?"

"Sometimes. They don't miss me much, Doctor Collins. In a way, that hurts. In another way, I'm thankful."

"And your husband?"

"I talk to him on the phone, too. He doesn't understand. About my trying to kill myself, I mean. He thinks maybe it's because he did something wrong. I try to tell him what you tell me. You know, that no one can make another person want to die. But Bill's like that. He's too responsible. That bothers me sometimes. Like, you know, Bill married me because I was pregnant. I was so dumb, Doctor Collins. I loved Bill. But how do I know he loved me? And now I wonder if I really did love him. He seems like a different person now."

"In depression, love is a sad thing, Elsa. The depressed person pities himself. He hates himself. He blames himself. The depressed person sees the love of others as pity. He can't give love freely. He can't accept it either. He fights with the people he used to love. He makes them feel self-conscious. They begin to question their love for him."

"Aren't you supposed to question love? Women complain that their husbands take them for granted." Elsa put out her cigarette. She took another from her pack and lit it.

"It's OK to take married love for granted. And love for one's children. That is one of the comfortable aspects of married life. You take for granted everyone in the family loves everyone else. It doesn't matter why you married, Elsa. Love should be comfortable. A habit. Not a puzzle. Not a constant surprise. Depression makes you feel unlovable. And it makes you see others as unloving."

"Maybe that explains my affair with Don. You see, Don was crazy about me when we were young. That sounds conceited. But I know he was. When I met him by chance a few months ago, I could see on his face that he still cared. It helped me for a while to think that he loved me.

67

"I can see now that I went outside my marriage because I felt bad about myself. I probably drink for the same reason."

"I'm glad you know that, Elsa."

"Doctor Collins, patients on the ward say talking doesn't help. They say it's the medicine that cures you."

"That's true."

"But talking does help! I feel better after I talk with you."

"Everybody needs to talk things out. If you keep on taking your medicine and we talk together, well, then we'll be getting someplace."

Dr. Collins hesitated a moment. "There's one thing more, Elsa. Something that medicine and talking don't fix."

"What's that?"

"Your drinking. A chapter of Alcoholics Anonymous meets here in the hospital. Join. Attend meetings even after you leave here."

"I'm not an alcoholic."

"Maybe not. But if you drink, you'll get depressed again." Dr. Collins rose as if to dismiss Elsa. Elsa remained seated. "Is there something else?" Dr. Collins asked.

"You have no right to tell me what to do," Elsa said. Her voice sounded childish to her. Its tone embarrassed her. Then, almost in spite of herself, she added, "I used to like you, Doctor Collins. Now I don't."

Dr. Collins spoke softly. "You don't have to like me, Elsa. We can work together anyway. But, if you decide you don't want me as your doctor, you can change doctors. That's your right."

Elsa wanted to cry out, No, no, no. I want you as my doctor! But her pride wouldn't let her say that. She gave in just a little bit. "I'll look into Alcoholics Anonymous. But I might not join."

Chapter 13

Elsa started acting strangely on the ward. Sad, quiet, grown-up Elsa became a brat. She found pleasure in behaving like a willful child. She never said yes if she could say no. She was never prompt if she could be late. She never soothed if she could snap. Elsa was mad at the world.

Mrs. Rose brought the children on Saturday afternoon. Dr. Collins gave permission for Elsa to meet them in the lobby. Mrs. Rose flopped into an armchair. Abby sat on her lap. "Don't wander off," Mrs. Rose called to Kevin and Katie.

"Mother," Elsa said, "the children are in sunsuits. Why didn't you bring sweaters for them? It's twenty degrees colder in here than outside."

"I didn't think of it, Elsa. My, don't you look a lot better! You must have gained a few pounds."

"The medicine does it."

Kevin and Katie came running. They threw themselves against Elsa. "When are you coming home?" Kevin asked.

A lump formed in Elsa's throat. She felt like kneeling down and embracing the children. She wanted to cry. Instead, to her own horror, and the children's, she heard herself say, "What do you care? You don't need me. Katie, let go. You'll tip me over."

The visit did not last long. Back on the ward, Elsa wept.

"I'm worse," she told Dr. Collins. "I used to be pathetic. Now I'm downright mean."

"It's temporary," Dr. Collins said. "You've lost some of your crutches. Liquor and suicide plans. Negative as they were, they gave you support. The anger was always in you. You used to turn it on yourself. Now you are turning it on others. You'll soon learn how to handle your anger. You'll work it off. Or laugh it off. Or change what makes you angry. Have you gone to AA yet?"

"No. I'm not a real alcoholic, Doctor Collins."

"Go anyway. They deal with feelings like these."

Elsa decided she might as well go. She was amazed at her first AA meeting. Why, she thought, these people are just like me. The people at AA understood her depression. Her anger. Her fear. Her suicide attempt. Most of them had been down the same road. A lot of them were divorced. Some of them had attempted suicide more than once. Some were physically ill. Others had been in and out of psychiatric wards.

"You're lucky," a woman named Polly told Elsa. "You're getting good help young. As you grow older, you'll find ways to help yourself. If you become depressed again, you won't drink. You won't have affairs. You won't attempt suicide. You'll go for help early on. You won't let depression ruin your life. I wish I were your age again. Knowing what I know now, I mean."

* * *

As the weeks passed, and the medicine took hold, Elsa's anger seemed to drain away. She began to feel peppy again. She began to miss Bill and the children. She thought of friends at home. She wondered what was happening in her neighborhood. She felt the need for work. I bet the house hasn't had a good cleaning since I left, she thought.

"Hey," she joked with Dr. Collins, "I've been in your booby hatch almost two months. I want out."

"All right," Dr. Collins agreed. "I'll miss you. But I'm glad you feel like leaving. I'll give you the name of a psychiatrist in your town. Call him as soon as you get home. I'll send him your records. Stay on the medicine until he takes you off."

"I hope the next doctor is as nice as you."

"I thought you didn't like me."

"I didn't for a while. You took away things I thought I needed. That was hard. But I like you now. Myself, too. Thanks a lot."

"Psychiatrists only show the way. The patient has to help himself."

"I know that now. But when you're depressed, it's hard to find the way."

* * *

Elsa didn't like the hometown psychiatrist as much as Dr. Collins. Dr. Scott monitored her medicine. But he didn't take time to talk much. At first Elsa was disappointed. Then, one day, leaving his office, she had a new thought. Why do I have to talk to a doctor? she asked herself. I can talk to Bill. And to the people at AA. And to my friends.

And I can listen to them, too. When I was sick, I wasn't tuned in. I didn't really listen to anybody. I'm not on an island anymore. I'm back on the mainland. With other people. They hear me. I hear them.

Elsa pulled out a pack of cigarettes. She put one in her mouth. As a person among people, I can make my own decisions, she thought. I can decide what's good for me. She was about to light the cigarette. But she blew out the match. She took the cigarette out of her mouth and stared at it. "Bill doesn't like you," she told the cigarette. "The kids don't like you. My mom doesn't like you. You're bad for me. Why do I put up with you?"

She again put the cigarette into her mouth. What am I doing? she asked herself. Am I waiting for a doctor to tell me to stop smoking? What if a doctor never does? Why can't I tell myself to stop?

At the corner was a waste can. Elsa took the package of cigarettes from her pocket. The matches, too. She carefully put the loose cigarette back into the package. Then she pitched them. "Goodbye, darlings," she told the cigarettes, now in the can. "I'll miss you. But I'm better off without you."

Chapter 14

The calendar showed January 5. The clock said 9:15. Elsa heard the tires of Bill's truck crunch snow in the driveway. The motor was turned off. Then came the sound of Bill's boots on the porch.

Elsa plugged in the sandwich grill and put the tea kettle on to boil. She took plates, cups, and saucers out of the cupboard. She laid two places at the kitchen table.

"Wow! Is it ever cold out there!" Bill said as he kissed Elsa.

"The forecast says zero by morning."

"Um, something smells good. What is it tonight?"

"Grilled ham salad sandwiches. We had that ham left over from the party on New Year's Eve. I ground it up with pickles and eggs. The kids loved it." Because she felt good, Elsa laughed.

Bill put his arms around Elsa from behind. "Honey, it's good to hear you laugh again. That laugh used to be your trademark. It says 'I'm happy.'"

"You weren't laughing much yourself for a while."

"I know. Your depression depressed me. You got so damn touchy, I dreaded coming home at night. I worried all the time. Maybe I'll cross Elsa. Maybe I'll do the wrong thing. Maybe she's tired of me. Maybe I'm as boring as I suspect I am. Maybe—. Well, you know, once a guy starts worrying that way, he's uptight for sure. If you hadn't gone to visit your mom, I would have visited mine."

Elsa turned in Bill's arms. "Oh no, you wouldn't. I know you. Lucky for me, you're too responsible to ever leave a wife. Have I ever said thanks, Bill? Thanks for being just the way you are?"

The teakettle's whistle drew them apart. While Elsa saw to the food, Bill fished small metal pieces from his pants pocket. "I finally came across some parts I think will fix that broken stroller," he said.

"Find something to put them in. They'll get lost if you leave them on the counter."

Bill looked around. "How about that bandage box on the windowsill?"

"No, not that."

"It's empty, isn't it?"

Elsa thought a minute. "No, it may look empty, but it's really full."

"Of what? Air?"

"It's full of hope. When I was a little girl, I had a book of Greek myths. One of them was the story of Pandora. A god, disguised as a man, left Pandora a box. He warned her not to open it. But Pandora did open the box. Out of the box flew all the ills of the world. Pandora couldn't put them back. But one thing remained in the box: hope. That story was the Greeks' way of saying that no matter what befalls a person, he'll survive if he still has hope."

"I guess that was the worst part of your depression. I guess you lost hope."

"Yes. I planned to kill myself. I carried pills to Florida in that box. When I came out of the hospital, I found the box under the bed. I had knocked it off the nightstand in my attempt."

"Doesn't say much for your mother's cleaning."

"What do you expect? A woman her age being left with three little kids! If she kept *them* clean, she was doing well. Anyway, when I found the box, I had a sort of revelation. I said to myself, 'When that box was full of pills, it was empty of hope.' So I brought it back with me. I put it here in the

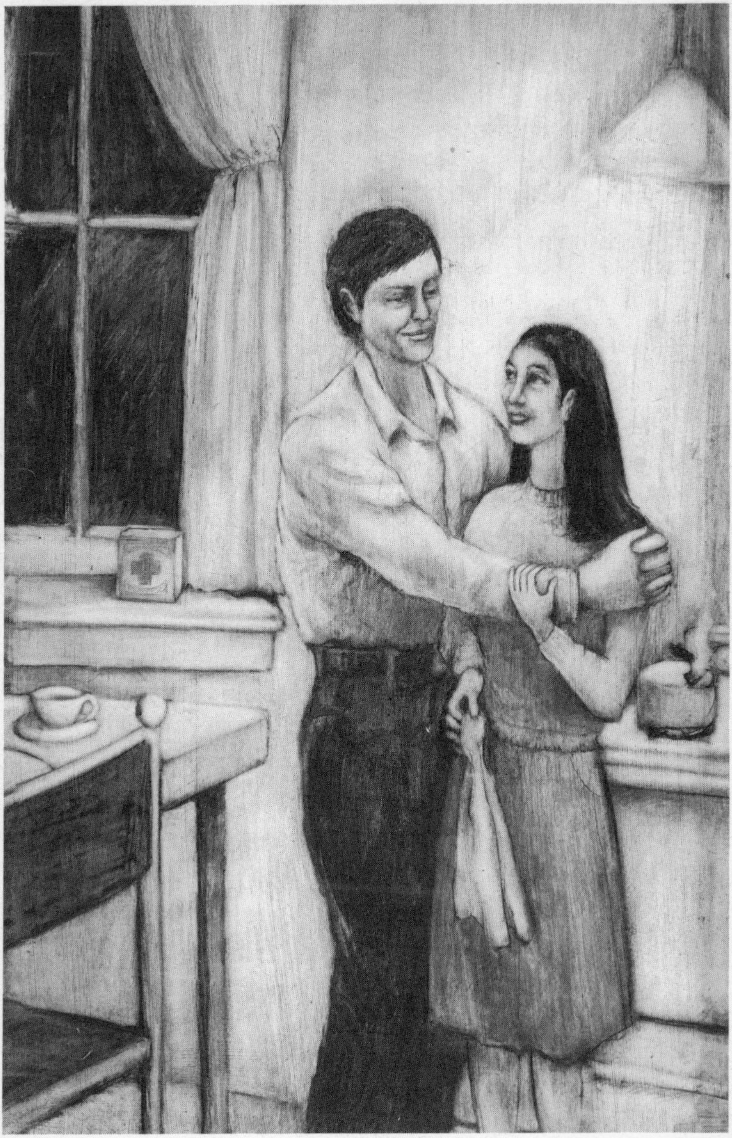

kitchen to remind me of what I learned in getting well."

"Like what?"

"It reminds me that saving pills is sick. That liquor is not medicine. That hope is not lost forever. No matter how completely you lose hope, you can get it back in time."

"I see," Bill said. For a moment his mouth twisted as if he were about to cry. Then he clapped his hands loudly and, with a laugh, said, "Come on, woman. Let's eat!"